TEAM HERO

Special thanks to Michael Ford

ORCHARD BOOKS

First published in Great Britain in 2019 by The Watts Publishing Group

1 3 5 7 9 10 8 6 4 2

Text © 2019 Beast Quest Limited
Cover and inside illustrations by Dynamo
© Beast Quest Limited 2019

Team Hero is a registered trademark in the European Union
Series created by Beast Quest Limited, London

A CIP catalogue record for this book is available from the British Library.

ISBN 978 1 40835 560 2

Printed in Great Britain

The paper and board used in this book are made from wood from responsible sources.

Orchard Books
An imprint of Hachette Children's Group
Part of The Watts Publishing Group Limited
Carmelite House, 50 Victoria Embankment, London EC4Y 0DZ

An Hachette UK Company
www.hachette.co.uk
www.hachettechildrens.co.uk

TEAM HERO

THE NIGHT THIEF

ADAM BLADE

ORCHARD

MEET *TEAM HERO* ...

JACK

POWER: Super-strength
LIKES: Ventura City FC
DISLIKES: Bullies

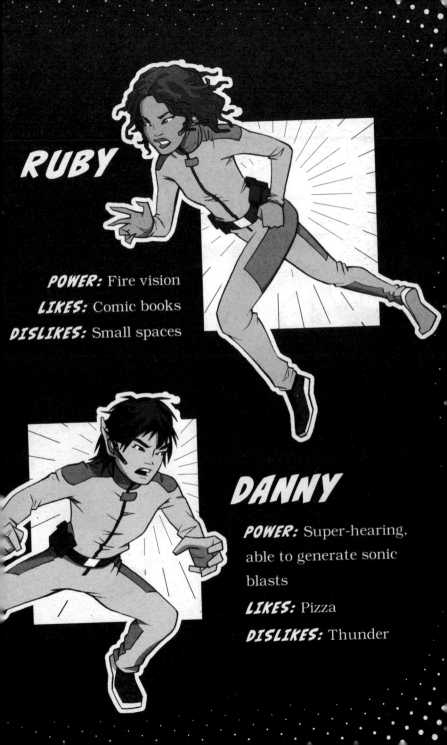

RUBY

POWER: Fire vision

LIKES: Comic books

DISLIKES: Small spaces

DANNY

POWER: Super-hearing, able to generate sonic blasts

LIKES: Pizza

DISLIKES: Thunder

CONTENTS

FLAMES ENGULFED the lower
part of the building, licking hungrily
up the sides. Steel melted under
the intense heat, glass splintered
and fell, and smoke belched from
the shattered windows. Below,
in the streets, cars lay smashed
and overturned, and people ran
screaming in all directions.

But there was nowhere to go.

Everywhere was the same. Rubble and dust clouded the air. Fires raged across the city, too many to ever be put out. Bridges collapsed into the river ...

Chancellor Rex lowered his arms and sagged back into a chair, exhausted. Projecting images of the future was a power he'd trained over many years, but it still took all his mental and physical energy.

"What does it mean?" asked Professor Yokata over the video link. She was standing in a jungle clearing.

After the Hero Academy

headmaster had caught his breath, he shook his head sadly and sighed.

"It means we haven't managed to stop the Agent raising the Hidden Army," he said. "The end of the world as we know it is still coming."

On the screen in front of him, beside Yokata, Jack appeared. The boy with the super-strong hands was only twelve, but he had already proved himself one of the bravest students that Hero Academy had ever produced.

"Chancellor, we've managed to get the second piece of the compass before the Agent," said the boy. "I

thought he couldn't find the Hidden

Army without it?"

"I don't understand either," said

Chancellor Rex. "What's clear is that we can't risk the Agent locating the third and final fragment."

"Then we'll find it first," said Jack, his jaw tightening. Rex saw the two other students in the background, Danny and Ruby. Her presence reminded him of their other problem — Ruby's mother, Dr Jabari, had been poisoned by the Agent's mysterious metallic compound, Xanthrum.

"I've requested the nearest Team Hero outpost send a specialist medical team to your location," said the Chancellor. "How is Dr Jabari faring?"

Professor Yokata looked grim. "She

is in a critical condition," she said. Then she lowered her voice. "I don't know how much longer she can hold on."

"No need to whisper," said Ruby, casting a sideways glance. "I might not have Danny's super hearing, but I'm not stupid. I know it's bad."

Rex had seen Ruby Jabari's courage first-hand on many occasions, but still he was worried about her. "Just hold on," he said. "Help will be there soon. For now, concentrate on the mission. Find that third piece of the compass. The world is depending on you all."

Yokata cut the video link and

Chancellor Rex stared at the blank screen, lost in his thoughts. Three students and a teacher were all that defended the world against the apocalypse. It seemed an impossible task.

"But if anyone can succeed, it's Jack and his friends," he muttered.

CHAPTER 1

AWAKENING

WATER DRIPPED from a crack in the domed ceiling high above. It spattered across the stone mezzanines, bridges and stairs that made up the vast chamber. But what had been a dark and dank ruin was now lit up with floating fluorescent lights, brought in by the archaeologists and other

specialists working for Team Hero.
They were there to gather intelligence
about the lost Taah Lu city, and the
Hidden Army who had fought them
five thousand years ago.

Jack and his friends watched the
specialists work, snapping photos
of the elaborate carvings on the
walls and measuring the crumbled
buildings.

There was particular interest in
the strange metallic pieces scattered
across the floor near to where Jack
and his friends stood — the remains
of a Soldier of the Hidden Army.
Plates and cogs, blades and gears

made of silver and gold, all piled up in disarray. Jack shuddered to think what the deadly machine would have looked like when fully assembled.

"I wish Mum could see all this," said Ruby sadly. "She's spent her whole life studying the Taah Lu."

"She'll get better soon," said Danny. "Dr Poe knows what he's doing."

They all turned to where the Team Hero physician was examining Dr Jabari. She looked completely normal but for one thing — the metallic film that coated her eyes. *Xanthrum*. Jack knew little about the exotic substance other than that it was deadly, and that the Agent seemed to have an endless supply. In small doses, it could make a person powerful, but over time could poison you. No one knew how long Dr Jabari had left if they couldn't find a cure.

"Small steps," encouraged Dr Poe. "Your heart rate is high."

Dr Jabari stumbled and collapsed into his arms.

"Mum!" cried Ruby, rushing forwards.

Dr Poe lowered Ruby's mother on to a stretcher.

"It's all right," said Dr Jabari. "I think I just overdid it. Come closer, Ruby." Jack's friend stood by the stretcher and took her mother's hand.

"I'm right here, Mum," she said.

Dr Poe was monitoring a tablet with his patient's vital signs, and Jack didn't like the worried frown on his face.

He doesn't know any more about

Xanthrum than the rest of us.

Above them, a group of archaeologists were working on a hovering scaffold, documenting a large section of the chamber wall that was covered in carvings. Jack had seen enough of the scenes of chaos already. The images showed ranks and ranks of spherical objects bristling with blades and other weapons, sweeping across the land, leaving crumbled towers, flattened trees, and terrified people in their wake. A wave of merciless terror and destruction that had eventually wiped the Taah Lu off the face of the earth.

And it'll do the same to us, if we

don't stop the Agent.

Jack's heart felt hollow. They'd triumphed over the Agent twice already, but it looked like those victories meant nothing, if the Chancellor's vision was correct.

"Someone's coming," said Professor Yokata, and her hands fell to the blaster pistols holstered at her hips. Jack looked towards the entrance to the cavern, but when two figures in Team Hero uniforms appeared, he breathed a sigh of relief. It was Madison and Simon, fellow students from the Academy.

"What have we missed?" said Simon.

"Quite a lot, actually," said Danny. "Any luck with your search?"

Madison shook her head as she approached. She and Simon had visited a nearby Taah Lu site to look for the third piece of the ancient compass. "The place was full of tourists," she said. "But we checked everywhere and there was no sign."

"Did you hear that?" asked Danny, jerking his head suddenly. The tips of his bat-like ears were twitching.

Everyone turned around, but there was nothing out of the ordinary. Ruby was still holding her mother's hand, while Dr Poe tapped away at his tablet.

"Maybe it was noth—" Danny began.

Suddenly Dr Jabari's body spasmed on the stretcher, her back arching. One hand shoved Ruby in the chest, throwing her through the air. Dr Poe stepped back in alarm. Dr Jabari sat up suddenly, her body rigid, then swung her legs off the stretcher.

"What's happening?" asked Danny.

Jack edged forwards, his hand dropping instinctively to the hilt of his sunsteel sword, Blaze. Dr Jabari's eyes were glowing more brightly than before, as if the Xanthrum itself was powering her movements. She set her feet down and began to stride towards the Soldier's metallic fragments.

"Mum?" said Ruby, picking herself up. She shot a panicked glance at Dr Poe. "What's wrong with her?"

Dr Poe shook his head, then glanced at the tablet once more. "Her heartbeat's spiking. I don't get it. She shouldn't even be able to stand."

At the edge of the pile of debris, Dr Jabari dropped to one knee and laid both hands on the ground. Jack gasped as he saw silver rivulets of Xanthrum trickle from beneath her fingertips and thread their way under the metal objects. The silver sheen in her eyes immediately faded and the pallor of her skin brightened to a healthier colour.

"The poison's leaving her!" said Ruby, grinning.

That's good, thought Jack, *but where's it going?*

From within, the pile stirred, as if something inside it was coming alive.

"Uh-oh," said Danny.

Ruby reached her mother's side and folded her in an embrace. The metal objects began to tremble.

"I think we should get back," said Jack.

Ruby pulled her mother away.

The first of the metal plates rose, scraping from the pile, levitating.

Others joined it, rotating in the air. Cogs and gears hovered then clanked together, locking into place. Slowly Jack realised what was forming — a limb, three metres long at least — a complex array of moving parts. *The arm of a Soldier of the Hidden Army!*

The scientists across the chamber all stopped what they were doing and came closer to the strange sight.

Dr Poe stepped back with wide eyes and Ruby helped her mother back on to the stretcher as the final pieces of the arm fastened in place with a hydraulic hiss. A huge fist at the end unflexed, but instead of fingers its

hand became a spinning circular saw.

I have a bad feeling about this!

"Get out, everyone!" Jack shouted.
The arm pivoted at the sound of his
voice, blades spinning. Then it lurched
towards his face.

CHAPTER 2

POINTING THE WAY

JACK DUCKED and the whirring blade passed over his head, embedding itself in the wall at his back. With a shrieking, grinding sound, it tore free and swung around. He drew Blaze, his sunsteel sword.

Bang! Bang!

Sparks flew as the arm jerked, and

Jack saw Professor Yokata had her blaster pistols in her hands. But when the smoke from the shots cleared, the Soldier's arm was undamaged. Jack couldn't see how it was able to hover in the air — maybe it was the Xanthrum — but it rose above them, cutting into the next level of the building, which showered rocks down. Ruby, still beside her mother, lifted her mirrored shield to protect them both as the debris fell. Danny unslung his bow and lined up an energy arrow. He fired but missed, and the whole chamber rumbled.

"Be careful!" said Yokata. "This

complex is unstable. We could bring the whole roof down."

Dr Poe pressed a button underneath the gurney and its legs folded up beneath, with jets keeping it airborne. "I'll get Dr Jabari to safety," he said, and began pushing the stretcher towards the exit passage. The Soldier's arm seemed to sense the movement, and swooped down over Jack's head towards the fleeing doctor. Ruby let loose a beam of fire from her eyes, which met the arm and slowed it down. Jack saw its surface glowing red with heat as it pressed on towards Ruby's mother, the metal blades spinning.

"I can't stop it!" Ruby cried. Her beams were growing weaker.

Jack jumped forwards, the heat bathing his face, and slammed the edge of Blaze into the arm. It spun around to face him, the red hot glow fading.

"Hey, come and get me!" yelled Madison.

The arm rotated towards the sound of her voice and more razor-sharp blades bristled along its length like the spines of a monstrous fish. Madison was waving her arms. "Catch me if you can," she said, then turned and sprinted away.

The Soldier's arm shot after her, and Jack saw straight away his fellow student wouldn't make it. She darted to one side but met the wall, spinning to face the deadly limb with nowhere to go. The arm paused for a moment, and Jack's heart was in his mouth. Then the spinning blades lurched forwards and buried themselves in her chest. But Madison didn't cry out or so much as flinch. She laughed as the arm passed right through her, and Jack realised he'd forgotten her special power. *Of course!* Madison could project images of herself. The arm seemed to learn too, though, and turned its attention back towards where Dr Poe was guiding Dr Jabari's stretcher to safety. It moved through the air stealthily, ignoring Madison's taunts.

The arm had almost reached the stretcher again when Simon's two arms stretched out like rubber and he wrapped his hands around it, carefully avoiding its deadly defences. He gritted his teeth.

"I can't hold it for long!"

Jack hacked and hacked at the metalloid limb, showering sparks everywhere. The arm shrieked and

slashed at him with the blades along
its length, but Jack put everything
into his blows. Aided by Ruby's
flames, Danny's energy bolts and
Professor Yokata's pistol shots,

they finally succeed in cracking
the armour cladding to reveal the
complex joints and gears beneath.
Jack drove Blaze into the depths
of the machinery and pressed his
weight into the hilt, prising at the
inner workings until they snapped
apart. The arm twisted back towards
his face, blades churning, but Jack
managed to grab the contraption's
"wrist". Focusing all his power into his
scaled fingers, he felt the metal give
in his grip, and the blades slowed. The
remains of the arm collapsed, falling
apart into pieces. A pool of Xanthrum
spread from beneath the wreckage.

Everyone flopped to the ground.

"We did it," said Ruby.

Only just, thought Jack. *And that was just one arm, of one Soldier.*

"I wouldn't want to meet a whole army like that," said Danny, speaking for everyone.

"And that's why our mission is so important," said Dr Jabari. "We need to find the next compass piece before the Agent does."

Jack saw that Ruby's mother was sitting up on her stretcher and he could hardly believe how energetic and healthy she looked.

"Mum!" said Ruby, throwing herself

into her mother's arms. "You're better."

"Just about, I think," said Dr Jabari, hugging her daughter tightly. "It looks like the Soldier drew the toxins from my body to power itself."

Slowly, the scientist and archaeologists began to return to the chamber. As some gathered around the remains of the Soldier arm, the others resumed their work recording the carvings.

"We're back to square one," said Simon. "The site we looked at had been stripped of anything valuable ages ago. The Agent could have found the next piece of the compass already."

"I don't think he has," said Dr Jabari. "One piece is supposed to lead to the next, and we have the second piece."

Jack took the oddly shaped shard of stone from his pocket. During his last battle with the Agent, he'd found it on a statue in this very room. The fragment had a few worn engravings, and nothing else. "It's not saying much to me," he said glumly.

"Can anyone read the symbols?" said Danny.

They all gathered closer and passed

the fragment around, frowning.

Danny held it to his ear, as if it might talk to him, and Ruby brushed her fingers across its surface.

"There must be some way to activate it," she muttered. "An on switch or something like that ..."

Activate it ... thought Jack. *Like the Xanthrum brought the arm to life ...*

"I've got an idea," he said, and held out his hand for the compass piece.

Ruby gave it back to him, and Jack walked over to the remains of the arm and crouched down beside the pool of Xanthrum on the ground.

"Be careful," said Professor Yokata.

"That stuff's deadly."

Jack took one end of the compass and dipped it gently in the liquid metal. As soon as the stone touched the Xanthrum, blue veins, invisible a moment before, began to spread across the symbols like neon ink seeping from within the stone.

Jack felt a tug and the piece of the compass shot from his hands, floating up into the air. Then it rotated slowly, its sharper end wobbling for a moment, before fixing in position.

"It's pointing!" said Ruby.

"Hawk," said Jack, excitement bubbling. "Can you plot the direction the fragment is indicating?"

"Very straightforwardly," said his Oracle. *"It's pointing 3.754 degrees north of eastwards."*

"And that is?" asked Jack.

"A direct line to Baotecca City," said

Hawk. *"Eighty-two kilometres away."*

"Baotecca is a huge place," said Professor Yokata. "Three million inhabitants. Hard to know where to start looking."

Jack's hopes dimmed, but Dr Jabari spoke up. "I think we can narrow it down," she said. "Baotecca Museum has the world's greatest collection of Taah Lu artefacts. It could be that the third piece of the compass was found on the site Madison and Simon visited but ended up in the museum."

Simon's elastic arm snatched the compass piece from the air. "Baotecca City, here we come," he said.

CHAPTER 3

MISSION TO BAOTECCA

THE TEAM Hero river transport, the *Orca*, housed state-of-the-art navigation, communication and weapons systems. At the flick of a switch, it could convert to full submarine mode. As soon as they were out of sight of any habitations, Professor Yokata pushed the throttle to max, and they cut a. winding river at close to fifty knots. Soon they reached the outskirts of the thriving metropolis of Baotecca, and Yokata slowed the boat. They pulled up at one of the main wharves. The shoreline was filled with colourful shops and restaurants, and a band was playing clashing music accompanied by drums.

"Shame we're not here to party," said Jack.

"Stealth packs, everyone," said Professor Yokata.

She handed each of them what looked like a belt, and Jack looped his around his waist, then pressed the small switch near the buckle. His Team Hero bodysuit shimmered for a moment, before turning into a T-shirt and jeans. Danny suddenly appeared to be wearing a Baotecca City FC tracksuit and cap that covered his bat-like ears, and Ruby a pair of shorts with a short-sleeved top. Sunglasses concealed her orange eyes.

"I'll stay here and monitor the comms with Simon and Madison," said Professor Yokata. "We'll keep an eye out for the Agent. If you need backup, use your Oracles to call us."

Jack and his friends set off into the

bustling crowds, and they soon found their way to the old quarter of the

city. Up a wide set of stairs was the grand façade of the Baotecca Museum. Tourists climbed the steps towards the double doors, or paused for photos.

Danny and Ruby had already joined the throng and Jack set off after them. As they entered under the looming porch area of the museum and walked into a vast lobby, he asked his Oracle, "Hawk, can you show me a map of the layout, please? We need to find the Taah Lu exhibits."

"I don't know who Hawk is, young man," said a woman in an attendant's uniform. "But here's a plan of the museum.' She held out a leaflet. 'All the finds from the Parracudo jungle are on the second floor."

Jack blushed, thanked her and took the leaflet.

The route took them through a hall full of looming dinosaur skeletons, then a long gallery lined with suits of armour from medieval Europe. Jack would have loved to stop and take it all in, but they had a mission to complete. Ruby nudged his arm and pointed to a room, grinning. The sign above the door read: *"The Lost Civilisation of Solus: Fact or Fiction?"*

Jack smiled back. One of their previous quests had taken them to the city of Solus, hidden deep in the desert near the Team Hero outpost in Khalea. It was a magical place inhabited by four species of human-animal hybrids, and they'd saved it from the threat of a Noxxian invasion.

They were climbing the stairs when a man hurried past. "Keep up, keep up!" he said. Around his neck was a lanyard which read "*Guide*" and he was leading a party of schoolchildren. "The Taah Lu exhibit is just up here."

He could be useful, thought Jack, and he and his friends joined the group.

Some of the kids already looked bored, and one was flicking the ear of a girl with glasses. "Stop it, Harry!" she said, spinning around.

"Stop what, four-eyes?" sneered the boy.

Jack wanted to help, but the guide had begun speaking and he listened intently as they entered the gallery.

"The Taah Lu, whose cities

spread throughout the Parracudo jungle, disappeared around five thousand years ago. We've found remains of what appear to be extensive settlements, with evidence of a complex system of government. It appears the Taah Lu people had an understanding of astronomy, mathematics and advanced metalworking way ahead of contemporary civilisations in Europe and Asia. But then something happened: they disappeared. Archaeologists have shown that the fall of the Taah Lu was rapid. Within less than a year, all their cities were in ruins, and within a decade the jungle had swallowed all that remained."

The Hidden Army was to blame, thought Jack.

Ruby had already peeled away from the group to inspect the exhibits, and Jack went the other way. There were shards of ancient pottery, a few tools and finely crafted jewellery. It wasn't a huge room by any means though, and Jack had soon surveyed all the items on display.

"Any sign of the third compass piece?" Danny asked. He was standing in front of a model reconstruction of a temple just like the one in which Dr

Jabari had first been attacked.

Jack shook his head, then cast a glance about. "Let's see if the second piece points the way," he said.

Danny and Ruby crowded closer to him, to hide what he was doing. Jack took the compass piece out of his pocket. He could feel its strange pull straining in his hand at once, and let it hover in the air. For a moment it trembled, its veins glowing blue, then spun so that its pointed end faced directly down at the floor.

"What does it mean?" asked Danny.

"Hey!" said a voice, and a security guard with a beard and glasses strode

up to them. "What have you got there?"

Jack snatched the compass piece out of the air. "Just a toy," he said.

The guard tilted his head. "Well, this is a museum, not a playground," he said. "Where are your parents?"

"Er ..." said Ruby, looking worried.

"They're in the café," said Jack quickly. "Downstairs."

"Well, I think you should get back to them," said the guard. "I'll take you."

"It's OK," said Ruby. "We know the way."

They hurried from the Taah Lu gallery and back to the stairs. Jack could feel the suspicious guard still watching them the whole way.

"There must be a storage room underneath the main museum," said Ruby. "A place like this can't put everything on display. All we need to do is find it."

They passed the suits of armour.

"Time for that plan of the building, Owl," said Danny to his Oracle. "We need to know the areas not open to the public."

Jack saw the faint glimmer of a holographic map in front of Danny's face, beamed there by his Oracle.

"This way," Danny said, and led them along a side corridor, down another set of stairs, past some toilets, to a door marked "*Authorised Personnel Only*". There was a numerical keypad to gain access. Thankfully there was no one looking.

"I could break it," said Jack, lifting a

glowing hand.

"That would be inadvisable," said Hawk in his ear. *"The museum has several high-tech security protocols."*

Jack sighed. "Any ideas, then?"

"Of course. Shall I just hack the systems?" asked Hawk.

"Um, sure, if you can without—"

A green light appeared on the keypad, and the door clicked open.

"Thanks!" said Jack.

Checking no one was watching, they slipped through the doorway.

They found themselves in a wide corridor, with several doors off either side. Dull strip lights glowed along the

ceiling. Jack took out the compass
piece straight away and balanced it
on his palm. It spun to point down the
passage and he led the way. By the
fourth door, the compass piece began
to rotate.

"Through here," he said.

They entered a large space, filled
with a jumble of stored artefacts.
More glass cases; statues large and
small; chests; and paintings stacked
up against each other on the floor.
A large glass cabinet was filled with
carefully catalogued jewellery made
with an assortment of precious
metals, coloured stones and gems. It

wasn't just Taah Lu relics, Jack saw. Some of the statues looked Greek or Roman, and there were shelves of totems that might have been Native American. The compass piece slid from Jack's hand and pointed downwards again. He sighed.

"There must be another level beneath us," he said.

As they turned to leave, a figure blocked the doorway and they all gasped at once. It was just a silhouette until he stepped into the light. It was the security guard again.

"I knew you three were up to something," he said.

"We got lost," said Ruby quickly.

"And somehow bypassed the security door?" said the guard. "I don't think so. Now let's see that so-called toy of yours."

"We need to get back to our parents," said Danny.

The guard stepped further into the room. "You're not going anywhere," he said. Then he tapped something by his collar, and his face flickered and then changed.

Jack struggled to grasp what he was seeing. "Dr Poe!"

"One of my many masks," said the man. "But you can call me Fade."

He touched his belt and his uniform shimmered for a moment before being replaced with a sculpted combat suit. It didn't look like Team Hero gear.

He must work for the Agent!

The man lifted an arm, and from the wrist section of his suit extended a small energy blaster. "Give me the compass piece, or you'll all die."

Jack looked at his friends.

He shoved the compass piece back into his pocket. "No way," he said. "If you want it, come and take it."

Fade smiled cruelly. "I was hoping you'd say that."

With a snarl, he opened fire.

CHAPTER 4

TRAPPED!

THEY DEACTIVATED their stealth
packs and Ruby used her shield to
ricochet the blast into a glass cabinet.
Fragments crashed to the ground,
and spinning gemstones pattered over
Jack and his friends. Almost at once,
an ear-splitting alarm began to sound,
and red lights flashed across the

chamber. A grid of lasers blinked into life, barring the doorway and trapping them inside.

"No escape. Just you lot and me now," said Fade. He aimed again and fired. Jack grabbed Danny and pulled him behind a marble statue of a man fighting a snake.

Boom!

The statue's head flew off and bounced across the ground. Cracks snaked down through the marble figure.

Jack drew Blaze from his scabbard and Danny prepared an energy arrow.

Ruby, still crouched behind her

mirrored shield, looked furious. "I don't get it. You helped my mum!"

"It might have looked like that," said Fade, "but I was working for the Agent all along. He needed someone with my unique skills, and in return for this nice new combat suit, I was happy to oblige. Wait until you see what it can do! I brought Dr Jabari to the pieces of the Soldier because I knew it would draw the Xanthrum from her and let you activate the compass piece in order find the next one. Now, are you going to come out and play?"

"With pleasure," growled Danny.

He jumped out from their hiding place and roared a sonic blast. It slammed into Fade, knocking him back a fraction. But then his body seemed to turn almost transparent for a moment, and he regained his balance.

What's he made of? Jack wondered, worried that Fade had barely been affected by Danny's attack.

Still, while Fade was distracted, they had a chance. Jack picked up a shard of stone from the damaged statue and threw it at Fade. As the spy lifted his arms, Jack ran at him, stabbing with his blade. But Fade sidestepped deftly, and Jack tripped headlong into a stack of crates, which tumbled to the ground. He heard the zap of Fade's blaster and jerked sideways. The nearest crate exploded right where his head had been. Spinning to face Fade, he couldn't see his enemy anywhere.

"Where'd he go?" asked Ruby, peering out from behind her shield.

"Right here!" said Fade, appearing behind Danny.

How'd he do that?

"Duck!" said Ruby.

Danny obeyed, and Ruby's fire-beams burned into Fade's chest. The

combat suit glowed red hot, but
then the jet of flame passed straight
through him, into a picture hanging
on the wall that looked at least three
hundred years old. The canvas went
up in flames at once. Fade didn't look

bothered in the slightest, and lifted his blaster to shoot back. Jack moved quickly, slicing down at Fade's wrist. But again, the blade passed through him, and his enemy grinned. "You're beginning to see this fight is futile, aren't you?" Jack stepped back, and swung Blaze sideways. The sword met no resistance. *How can he be solid one minute, and like a ghost the next?*

Fade reached out and grabbed Jack around the neck, lifting him from the ground. "Are you going to give me the compass piece, or do I have to kill you for it?"

Jack balled his fist and punched Fade

in the side of the head. This time the blow connected, and Fade dropped him, stumbling off balance.

Danny released another sonic roar, and it threw Fade across the room. But instead of hitting the wall, he simply vanished through it.

Jack was breathing hard. "That combat suit lets him phase in and out of being solid," he said, "but he can't do both at the same time. The only way we'll defeat him is if we work together."

"You won't defeat me," came a voice from above.

Jack looked up and there was

Fade, his head and one arm poking through the ceiling, but no sign of his body. He fired his blaster, and they all dived for cover. Fade dropped into the room, landing nimbly on two feet. He fired again at Danny, who scurried out of the way. Then he picked up Ruby by the ankle to drag her out of hiding. Jack scrambled up and hurled himself at the slippery thief. He landed on Fade's back, wrapping an arm around his neck and squeezing hard. Fade dropped Ruby, then suddenly Jack's grip on him disappeared. He fell to his knees and saw Fade standing over him.

"Stop trying," he said. "This is just business. Give me the compass piece and no one has to get hurt."

"Never!" said Jack. He tried another punch, but it passed harmlessly through Fade's head, and Jack overbalanced. Next moment, Fade rushed him. Jack braced himself for the blow, but it never came. His enemy's body simply seeped through him, making Jack feel strangely seasick, like his insides were being tugged by an invisible force. Then Fade was beside him, and in his hand he held the second fragment of the ancient compass.

"How did you do that?" he asked.

Fade spun the compass piece around on his hand, and then it vanished.

"A magician never reveals his secrets," he said, turning and striding towards the wall. "Now I'll go and find the final piece while you three wait here for the real security to come."

"Stop him!" cried Jack. Danny fired an energy arrow, but it was too late. Fade had drifted through the wall and the arrow bounced off, bringing down a shower of stone and plaster dust.

"We have to get after him!" said Danny. He rushed for the doorway, only for Ruby to yank him back.

"Are you mad? You'll get fried!"

She picked up a scrap of glass and tossed it at the lasers criss-crossing the door. The glass exploded on impact, then melted into red globules on the floor.

"Well, we can't walk through walls," said Danny. "How do we get out?"

Jack went to the wall. "We can't walk through it," he said, summoning all his strength into his right fist. "But maybe we can knock it down."

He drew back his hand and thumped as hard as he could. The top layer of plaster and concrete crumbled, but he heard a metal

CRUNCH!

clang. "Hawk wasn't wrong about the security in this place. These walls are reinforced with steel!"

"Can you get through?" asked

Danny, frowning.

"It might take a while," said Jack. "And I'd be worried about bringing the ceiling down on us." He paused. "Hawk, can you kill the lasers like you opened the security door?"

"Negative," said his Oracle. *"This system is tamper-proof and can only be deactivated manually from the central control room."*

"I've got an idea," said Ruby, inspecting the frame of the doorway. "Maybe we can use the power of the lasers against themselves. Stand well back."

Jack and Danny did as she said.

Ruby joined them, then laid her mirrored shield on the ground. Jack understood what she was going to do. With her foot, Ruby nudged the shield hard across the floor, so it slid into the path of the white-hot bars. As soon as they touched the shield's surface and reflected back on themselves, splinters of light shot off in random directions. There were several loud bangs and explosions of sparks. Jack shielded his eyes. When the fizzing sound ceased he looked up through the smoke to see the lasers had short-circuited and the doorway was clear.

"Good work, Rubes!" said Danny. "We need to tell security that the vaults have been infiltrated by a master thief!"

The three friends rushed from the room, back along the corridor and burst out into the main part of the museum near the entrance lobby where visitors milled about. They stopped in their tracks.

Waiting for them was a semicircle of security staff, armed with Tasers.

"Freeze!" said the leader.

Behind the guards, people were being escorted from the museum by staff. Jack realised the alarms were sounding out here as well, though no one was panicking … yet.

"You have to get to the vaults!" said Jack. "There's a thief down there. His name is Fade and if he—"

"Be quiet!" said the guard. "You can't trick us. We're looking at the real thieves! Drop the weapons!"

Jack realised, too late, that he hadn't reactivated his stealth pack and Blaze was clearly visible at his side. He looked at Danny, armed with his bow, and Ruby with her shield.

We must look pretty suspicious!

"Please listen to us," said Danny. He stepped forward and raised his arms, but at the same moment a couple of impressive-looking gemstones fell from his sleeves. They must have landed there during the fight.

The guards all looked from the jewels to Danny.

"Uh – I know how that might look, but you have to hear me out ..."

"I think we've heard enough," said the leader. "Take them down, team!"

Jack saw fingers tense against their triggers and Ruby jumped up to block the Taser shots with her shield.

Then a window imploded and a figure flew through, hovering on jet-boots. Everyone froze in shock, taking in the cloaked figure floating three metres up.

The Agent!

From behind his reflective metal mask, he chuckled.

"I can't let any of you interfere with Fade's mission," he said, reaching

under his cloak and drawing out a gleaming silver orb.

A Xanthrum grenade!

"He has grenades!" Jack cried. "Take cover, everyone!"

CHAPTER 5

LIVING METAL

CHAOS BROKE out in the museum's great hall. Visitors began to scream and rush towards the exits.

It's a stampede, thought Jack. He shouted for calm, but no one could hear him.

There were still people running for the doors, but others spilled off into different parts of the museum. Jack watched them in despair.

The Agent tossed a grenade into the crowd, and Danny blasted it with a sonic vibration. The grenade veered off target, smashed into a wall and exploded with a pop, showering silver droplets down the wall.

The Agent doesn't care how many people he harms, thought Jack.

"Who is that?" asked the leader of the security staff.

"The real enemy," said Danny. "You need to get people to safety."

"And secure the vault," said Ruby. She shot twin fire-beams at the

Agent, who crossed his gauntleted hands in front of his face and absorbed the flames.

The guards were fanning out among the panicked visitors, shepherding them away. Others had rushed back into the staff area looking for Fade. *Not that they have much chance of stopping him,* thought Jack.

He saw the group of schoolchildren from earlier. Their guide had vanished, and they were halfway down the stairs to the great hall when they spotted the Agent and stopped, mouths agape. The Agent saw them too, and Jack saw his eyes twinkle behind his mask.

"Let's see how heroic Team Hero really are," he said.

Then he darted above their heads and drew out a blaster. He raked the ceiling above the children, making it crack apart. A huge chandelier trembled, about to fall. Using the strength in his hands, Jack shoved his way through the crowds, calling to the kids. "Get off the stairs! Quickly!"

The only person who heard him seemed to be the small girl in glasses Jack had seen before. She began to push and cajole her classmates, hurrying them down. But one person had frozen in terror, crouching on the ground. Jack saw it was the boy who'd been picking on the girl before. One of the chains holding the lighting array broke and the whole thing swung down. Once the second chain went, that was it. Jack didn't know if he could make it in time. But suddenly the girl rushed back up the stairs. She grabbed the boy by the shoulders and hauled him away, saying, "Come on, Harry!"

Then the chain snapped.

The girl looked up and screamed. Jack used his super-strong hands to vault off the banister and launch

toward the chandelier. Using his strength while he was in midair, he managed to nudge the colossal light fixture just enough that the boy and girl below him stayed clear of the impact. He landed just past the two as the chandelier crashed down in a burst of glass and dust.

"Thank you!" the girl said. "Who are you guys?"

"We're Team Hero!" said Jack.

"Is that why your hands are like that?" asked the girl. Danny and Ruby came rushing up. "And his ears? And her eyes?"

"I guess so," said Jack. "But you don't

need special powers to be a hero. You just saved that boy's life."

The girl blushed. "I just did what was right."

"Exactly," said Jack.

"The Agent's headed towards the medieval section," Danny interrupted.

Near the doors, the security staff were restoring some order, channelling visitors to safety through the exits.

"Let's get after him," said Jack. "If we can keep him away from here, we might be able to limit casualties."

"Good luck, Team Hero," said the girl.

Jack carefully picked his way between the pools of silvery Xanthrum around one of the dinosaur fossils, and then pushed open the double doors into the medieval exhibit. The Agent stood at the far end, right in plain sight.

"There's nowhere to run," said Jack. "Even if Fade finds the third compass piece, we're not letting you leave."

"Really?" said the Agent. "From where I'm standing, you're outnumbered."

"Your maths is rubbish," said Danny, echoing Jack's own thoughts.

"Yeah," said Ruby, her eyes ready to unleash fire. "Give up, you idiot!"

The Agent laughed, the sound muffled under his silver mask. Then he threw out both arms. Orbs of

Xanthrum shot out, hitting the ceiling and exploding. Jack took cover, but droplets of the strange fluid fell well clear of them, instead cascading on to the suits of armour lining the room.

"You missed us," said Jack. He walked cautiously forward, expecting a trick.

"I wasn't aiming at you," said the Agent, tapping at something on his wrist. "I was aiming at them."

Jack caught a movement to his left, and saw a suit of armour glistening with Xanthrum lift its stiff arm, which clutched a broadsword. It scythed down, and Jack stepped back as the massive blade bit into the floor. The suit of armour ripped the sword free and stepped off its pedestal.

"Uh-oh," said Danny. "We've got a problem."

Jack backed off and saw that all the suits of armour, at least ten, were coming to life. Some clutched swords, others had spears, crossbows, halberds or spiked maces on chains.

"As you can see," said the Agent, "I've been working on a new version of Xanthrum that can animate objects."

Two knights approached Jack. One had a spiked helmet and swung a mace. The other thrust at him with a

spear. Jack ducked and drew Blaze,
then swiped the blade into the midriff
of the first armoured man. The knight
clattered to the ground in pieces.
Jack deflected the spear point of the

second, then smashed the hilt of his sword into a helmeted head.

The sounds of clashing metal at his back told him that Danny and Ruby had joined the fight too. He saw a suit of armour fly through the air and collide with the wall, before falling in a disjointed pile of metal on the ground. Another, glowing red hot, stumbled blindly past as it melted. Jack thrust the point of Blaze into its chest, and it collapsed.

Suddenly two gauntleted metal hands wrapped around his middle and hoisted him off the ground with crushing force. Jack dropped Blaze and gripped the metal arms. His hands glowed with strength and he tore the grip free. Balling his fist, he sent the helmeted head spinning off the armoured shoulders.

Danny had pinned one opponent against the wall with his sonic cry, and now lined up an energy arrow and let fly. The armour exploded into pieces. Ruby stunned a warrior with a fire-beam, then rushed at another, ramming the edge of her mirrored shield into the joint of the plates behind its knees. It dropped to the floor, and she kicked it in the chest before leaping up and bringing the shield down on to its neck. Jack finished the final warrior with his sword, driving the blade through both chest armour and back-plating. Xanthrum leaked from its wounds, and it fell at his feet.

He saw ten piles of armour lying in pools of silver liquid. His friends were breathing hard.

Suddenly Fade's head appeared through a wall, followed by his body. "Did I miss the fun?"

"Never mind that," said the Agent. "Did you find it?"

Fade held up two compass pieces, fitted together. "Sure did! Do you want

me to kill these kids now?"

The Agent shook his head. "No need.
I have it well in hand." He tapped
again at a control on his wrist. "I'll
meet you at the ship."

What ship? thought Jack. Fresh
screams came from the main

museum lobby, and the floor began to shake. Suddenly people came running, stumbling over one another and glancing back over their shoulders.

Jack rushed against the tide, staring over their heads, and what he saw made no sense at all.

It was a T-Rex, or the T-Rex skeleton at least. Only now, it was alive! Its skull was coated in Xanthrum, and its jawbone snapped up and down. The creature was pounding along the gallery floor on bony claws, each step cracking the marble floor, and it was headed straight for them.

CHAPTER 6

DINOSAUR ATTACK!

"THE XANTHRUM has brought it to life!" cried Ruby.

"So now we have a dinosaur to fight as well?" Danny asked. "Great."

The museum's visitors ran to escape the rampaging beast.

The massive creature lumbered towards the fleeing visitors. One of the security guards fired his Taser, and it lodged in the beast's stubby forelimb. The T-Rex reached down and closed its teeth over the guard, who screamed. Without even chewing, the dinosaur swallowed its victim, and the guard tumbled down its throat, landing among its ribs.

The crowd parted and the T-Rex charged a path towards Jack and his friends. It tried to duck beneath the door but didn't bend far enough. Its massive skull smashed into the top of the frame, and for a moment it tottered on unsteady legs before crashing down on to its side.

"Not that smart!" said Danny.

"Get me out of here!" yelled the man trapped behind the ribcage.

Fade, Jack saw, was slipping easily through the crowd, heading for the museum exit.

"Stop Fade and get the compass pieces at all costs!" he shouted to his friends.

The spy began to move more quickly through the great hall, but then Jack saw the girl with glasses. She thrust out a leg, tripping Fade up. He fell flat on his face and the compass skittered across the ground, before disappearing among the feet of the other schoolchildren.

"Don't let him have it!" cried the girl.

Fade growled and picked himself up. "Give it to me!" he said.

He jumped among the children, shoving and pulling them roughly. "Who's got it? Hand it over now!"

He was so busy scrambling for the prize that he didn't see Ruby hurl her mirror shield at a column near the school group. The shield cut through the air past the children then ricocheted off the column to hit Fade right on the side of his head. His knees buckled and he fell to the ground.

"Useless!" roared the Agent as he

jetted through the air above them.

He dived towards the schoolchildren, brandishing a Xanthrum grenade. They all scattered in fear, and he landed beside the compass pieces where they lay on the ground. Jack was about to go after him when he saw the T-Rex was stirring again. He brandished Blaze over his shoulder, both hands glowing on the hilt, and stood his ground to give the fleeing museum visitors more time to escape.

"You've failed!" said the Agent, locking his piece of the compass into the other two. It looked like a miniature boomerang with three arms. The Agent slipped it inside his cloak. "Soon the Hidden Army will be mine. Turn and run, little hero."

Jack ignored him, and fixed his eyes on the sockets of the T-Rex. The beast began to charge, crushing the marble floor beneath its feet.

I can't turn and run. These people need me!

From the side, Danny bellowed a sonic cry, but it barely slowed the creature. Ruby's fire-beams cut a scorching path over his skull, but otherwise did no harm. Jack couldn't tell if it was the floor beneath his feet that was trembling, or his own knees. The beast was like a speeding truck thundering towards him. A truck with teeth and claws, fuelled with pure hatred, the Xanthrum gleaming over its bony features.

A fraction of a second before the teeth snatched him up, Jack spun, and

swung his blade with so much force
he feared it would shatter. The impact
of sunsteel on Xanthrum-coated bone
threw him to the ground. The T-Rex
staggered past, and when Jack looked

he saw he'd completely severed one of the creature's feet. It teetered off balance, crashing into one wall, then the other, before collapsing.

Further down the gallery, the schoolchildren cheered. But Jack's heart spiked.

"Where's the Agent?" he called to his friends.

"Is that the guy with the mask?" asked a security guard hiding behind column. "He just flew out to the sculpture garden."

Jack, Danny and Ruby rushed to give chase.

A handful of the visitors had taken

refuge among the abstract statues in the garden. But the strangest thing Jack saw there was a huge platform of metal, blinking with lights and satellite arrays and bristling weapons systems.

The Agent's base!

The Agent was seated in the centre, on a high-backed chair that looked like a throne. In his hands he held the compass.

"You're just in time to see me off," he said.

With a huge crash, the T-Rex careered through one of the tall museum windows, staggering out into the garden on its single working foot. People threw themselves out of its lumbering path. Below, the sides of the platform began to fold up and in on themselves like a piece of high-tech origami. Jack was torn. He had to stop the Agent, but he also couldn't let the T-Rex maraud among the people in the garden either.

"Stop him taking off!" he cried to his friends.

Jack sprinted along the steps and jumped at the dinosaur. He gripped the ribs and clambered up, using all his strength not to be thrown off as the dinosaur thrashed and reached back to snap with its teeth. But once he was on its back, the jaws couldn't reach him.

The skeleton bucked and jerked, but Jack held on.

Ruby was raking the hull of the Agent's craft with fire, and Danny shot arrow after arrow. Billowing smoke rose across the courtyard as the visitor started to flee back inside.

Lifting his sword, Jack drove the point into the uppermost of the dinosaur's vertebrae, where its spine joined the base of its Xanthrum-covered skull. With a wrench he cut through, and the car-sized head sagged and broke free, crashing to the ground. Jack slid off, hitting the ground hard as the headless skeleton tottered, then stumbled and fell. It careered straight into the side of the Agent's folding vessel. The gears of the hull screeched as the T-Rex's colossal torso prevented them from closing.

We've stopped him! thought Jack, getting painfully to his feet.

Ruby and Danny broke off their attack. Apart from strange fizzing sounds and crackles coming from the damaged craft, and groans of a few men who'd been freed from the T-rex's ribcage, silence reigned across the smoke-filled courtyard.

The museum's security staff pressed closer, as did Jack and his friends.

"Careful," called Jack to everyone. "The Agent is still—"

The cloaked figure of their enemy shot straight from his grounded vessel up into the sky on his jet pack.

"I'm going to destroy your puny world!" he yelled down to the garden. In his hand the completed compass spun and glowed. "And one broken ship isn't going to stop me."

Angling his body, he flew away at incredible speed over the buildings of Baotecca City and out of sight.

Jack looked at his friends in despair. "He has the compass," he said. "We failed." Behind them, smoke rose from

the broken windows of the museum. It looked a bit like one of the images Chancellor Rex had shown them, but it was nothing compared with what the Hidden Army would do when they were unleashed.

"Don't be hard on yourself," said a small voice.

Jack saw it was the small girl with glasses. She put a hand on his shoulder. "You saved hundreds of lives in there. You're a hero."

All around them, people began to nod and clap, until the whole courtyard was applauding.

Ruby stepped up. "She's right — and

remember, my mum's safe and well again too."

"Yeah," said Danny. "And the Agent might have the compass, but he hasn't found his army yet. There's still time."

The hopes of the crowd and his friends lifted Jack's heart a little. They were right. The Agent thought he'd won, but he hadn't yet. Jack wasn't going to give up. He and his friends would keep going no matter what.

Because that's what heroes do ...

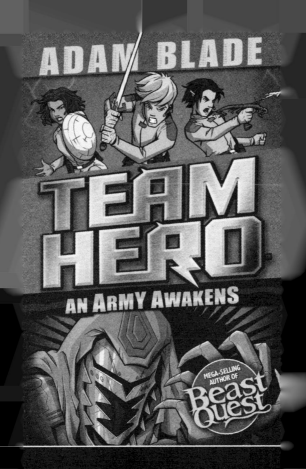

READ ON FOR A SNEAK
PEEK AT BOOK 16:

AN ARMY AWAKEN

CHAPTER 1

TRAPPED!

"WHAT A mess," Jack said, gazing around what was left of the sculpture garden of the Baotecca Museum. Jagged pieces of the museum's stone brickwork stuck up from the well-tended grass. Several sculptures had been flattened beneath fallen masonry.

At the centre of the wreckage hovered the Agent's base, a shining metal platform about the size of Jack's family's apartment in Ventura City — but Jack had seen it transform into many different shapes, even an aircraft. Ruby walked around the base, her orange eyes narrowing with interest as she inspected its strange devices and screens, all flashing with lights. The structure gave off an electrical static that set Jack's teeth on edge.

He and his friends had managed to capture the base, but only after the Agent's henchman, Fade, had stolen the final compass piece from the museum vault. Now the compass was complete, it could lead the Agent to a powerful mechanical army.

"What do we do?" Danny asked.

"We need to work out where the Agent's taking the compass, then stop him waking up the Hidden Army and destroying the world," Jack said.

Ruby turned away from the base, one eyebrow raised. "As plans go, that's pretty weak on detail," she said.

Check out the next book:
AN ARMY AWAKENS
to find out what happens next!

IN EVERY BOOK OF
TEAM HERO SERIES
FOUR there is a special
Power Token. Collect
all four tokens to get
an exclusive Team Hero
Club pack. The pack
contains everything you and
your friends need to form your
very own Team Hero Club.

MEMBERSHIP CARDS · MEMBERSHIP CERTIFICATE · STICKERS · POWER GAME · BOOKMARKS

Just fill in the form below, send it in with your four tokens
and we'll send you your Team Hero Club Pack.

SEND TO: Team Hero Club Pack Offer, Hachette Children's Books,
Marketing Department, Carmelite House, 50 Victoria Embankment,
London, EC4Y 0DZ.

CLOSING DATE: 31st December 2018

WWW.TEAMHEROBOOKS.CO.UK

- - - - - - - - - - - - ✄ - - - - - - - - - - - -

Please complete using capital letters *(UK and Republic of Ireland residents only)*

FIRST NAME
SURNAME
DATE OF BIRTH
ADDRESS LINE 1
ADDRESS LINE 2
ADDRESS LINE 3
POSTCODE ☐ ☐ ☐ ☐ ☐ ☐ ☐ ☐
PARENT OR GUARDIAN'S EMAIL

I'd like to receive Team Hero email newsletters and information about
other great Hachette Children's Group offers (I can unsubscribe at any time)

*Terms and conditions apply. For full terms and conditions please go to
teamherobooks.co.uk/terms*

*TEAM HERO Club packs
available while stocks last.
Terms and conditions apply.*

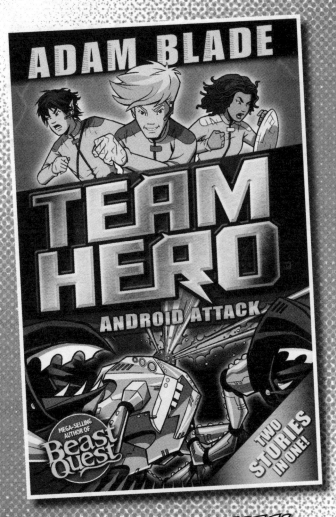

FIND THIS SPECIAL BUMPER BOOK ON SHELVES NOW!